To all my little monsters: may Dennis never eat you —B.G.

For Mo, who would have loved this book —T.K.

Farrar Straus Giroux Books for Young Readers
An imprint of Macmillan Publishing Group, LLC
120 Broadway, New York, NY 10271
mackids.com

Our books may be purchased in bulk for promotional, educational,
or business use. Please contact your local bookseller or the
Macmillan Corporate and Premium Sales Department at
(800) 221-7945 ext. 5442 or by email at MacmillanSpecialMarkets@macmillan.com.

Library of Congress Cataloging-in-Publication Data
Names: Gehrlein, Brian, author. | Knight, Tom, illustrator.
Title: The book of rules / Brian Gehrlein ; pictures by Thomas Knight.
Description: First edition. | New York: Farrar Straus Giroux, 2021. | Audience: Ages 3–6. | Audience:
  Grades K–1. | Summary: Presents a series of rules the reader must follow to avoid being eaten
  by Dennis the monster, including sitting on the floor crisscross-applesauce, making a fish face,
  and preparing to listen mindfully.
Identifiers: LCCN 2020016153 | ISBN 9780374314545 (hardcover)
Subjects: CYAC: Rules (Philosophy)—Fiction. | Monsters—Fiction. | Humorous stories.
Classification: LCC PZ7.1.G4473 Boo 2021 | DDC [E]—dc23
LC record available at https://lccn.loc.gov/2020016153

First edition, 2021
Book design by Cindy De la Cruz
Color separations by Bright Arts (H.K.) Ltd.
Printed in China by Hung Hing Off-set Printing Co. Ltd., Heshan City, Guangdong Province

ISBN 978-0-374-31454-5 (hardcover)
10 9 8 7 6 5 4 3 2

THE BOOK OF RULES

BRIAN GEHRLEIN

Illustrated by TOM KNIGHT

Farrar Straus Giroux
New York

THIS BOOK HAS RULES.

You must follow all the rules.
If you break the rules, Dennis will eat you.
Do you want to be gobbled by Dennis? No?
Then you'll have to listen carefully.

Come Here, Dennis!

Show them your teeth.

Now your claws.

Rule Number 1 — You Must Sit on the Floor

Are you nice and cozy?
Hmmm . . . that's
not quite right.

Find a new spot! Yes, that's better.
Actually . . . one more time!
Excellent job listening and following the rules.
You clearly don't want to be eaten.

Rule Number 2
SIT UP STRAIGHT

Sit up tall.
Sit crisscross applesauce.

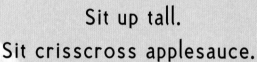

Applesaucier. APPLESAUCIEST! Nice.
Now, stay that way, and you won't
be Dennis-food.

Again, this time all together.
Give it your very best! Solid clapping.
We are very focused.

Rule Number 4
THE COW RULE

You are now required to moo like a cow. Moo like you mean it. Like a noisy barn! Udder-ly impressive.

Dennis never did like beef.

Rule Number 5
DO NOT SMILE!

Do not laugh. Do not even THINK about smiling or laughing.
There is nothing funny about being eaten.

Dennis!
They're breaking
the rules!

You really need to see a doctor about that foot.

Kids, looks like you're safe . . . for now.
Do not break the rules again.

Rule Number 6
MAKE A FISH FACE AT SOMEONE

Fishier!

LIKE THE FISHIEST FISH!

Well done, little fish.

We are swimmingly good listeners.

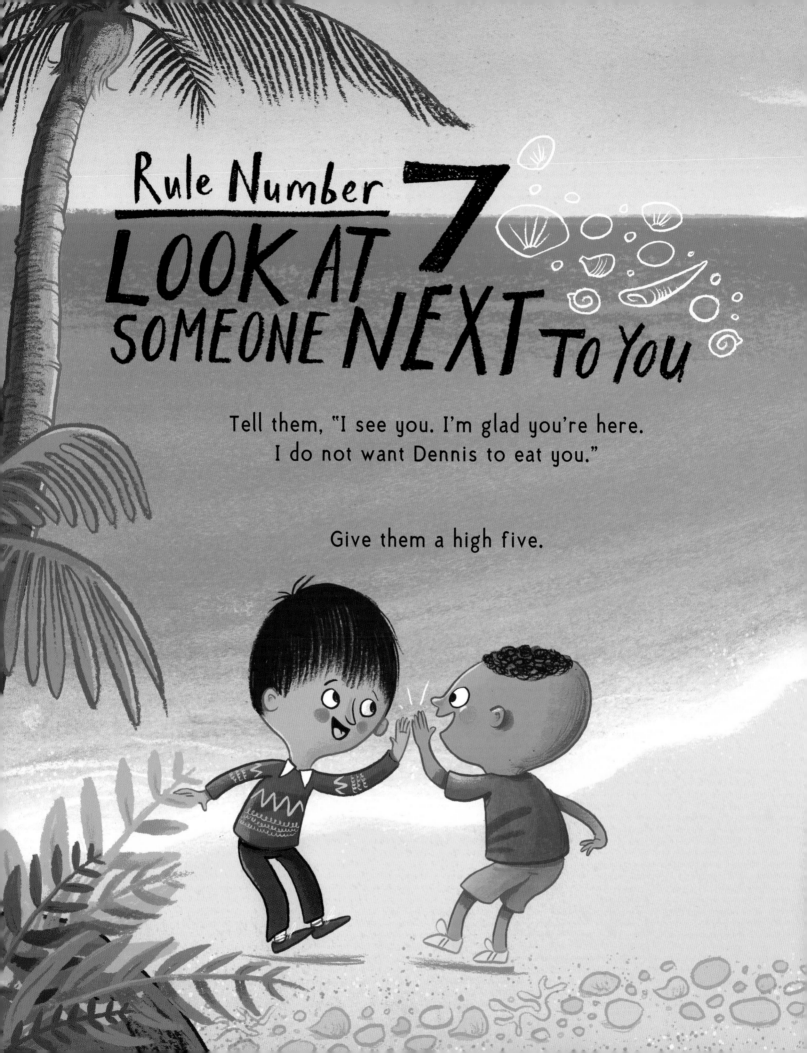

Rule Number 7

LOOK AT SOMEONE NEXT TO YOU

Tell them, "I see you. I'm glad you're here.
I do not want Dennis to eat you."

Give them a high five.

Fantastic. Dennis just might go hungry today.

Now a fist bump.

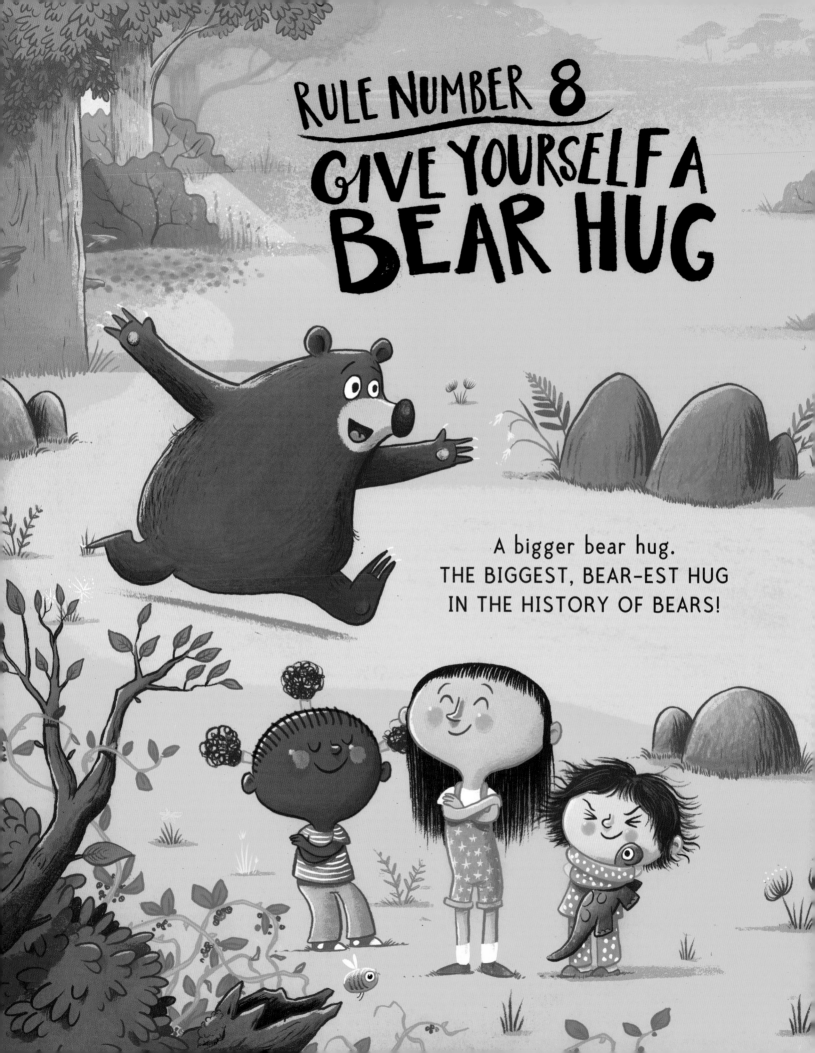

RULE NUMBER 8
GIVE YOURSELF A BEAR HUG

A bigger bear hug.
THE BIGGEST, BEAR-EST HUG
IN THE HISTORY OF BEARS!

And release. Good.
Bear-y good.
Perhaps too good to be eaten.

Rule Number 9
CLOSE YOUR EYES...

Don't worry—Dennis won't eat you.
Keep your eyes closed.

Feel your heartbeat.

Feel the floor.

Listen to the room.

Now breathe together.

Breathe in 1, 2, 3.
Breathe out 1, 2, 3.
Breathe in 1, 2, 3.
Breathe out 1, 2, 3.

Open your eyes. Perfect.

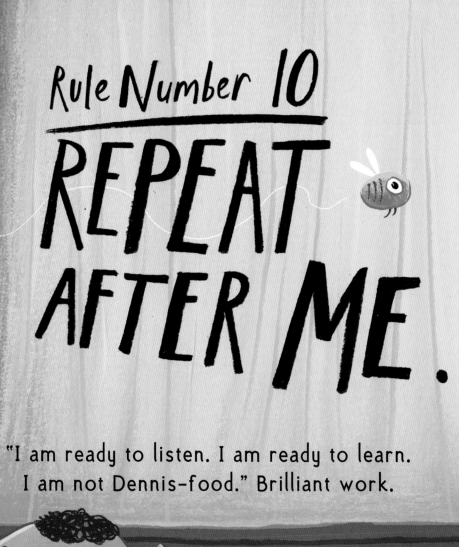

Rule Number 10

REPEAT AFTER ME...

"I am ready to listen. I am ready to learn.
I am not Dennis-food." Brilliant work.

You made it. You all made it.
Great job, everyone. You all listened
well and followed the rules.

No lunch for Dennis . . . unless
we follow the secret rule.
The rule we follow when
Dennis has nobody to eat.

COME OUT HERE, DENNIS...

Your whole body, not just your foot.

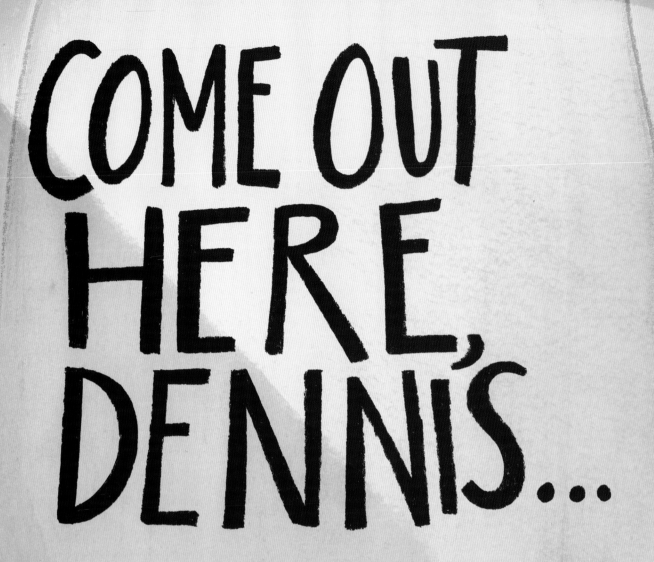

Do you want to know the secret rule?
You do?

Rule Number 11

FEED DENNIS ...

THE BOOK OF RULES!